Mike Swan,
SINK or SWIM

Mike Swan,

SINK or SWIM

by Deborah Heiligman
illustrated by Chris Demarest

A Yearling First Choice Chapter Book

For Benjamin, who goes for it
—D.H.

Published by
Bantam Doubleday Dell Publishing Group, Inc.
1540 Broadway
New York, New York 10036
Text copyright © 1998 by Deborah Heiligman
Illustrations copyright © 1998 by Chris Demarest
All rights reserved.

Library of Congress Cataloging-in-Publication Data
Heiligman, Deborah.
    Mike Swan, sink or swim / Deborah Heiligman : illustrated by Chris
Demarest.
        p. cm.
    Summary: Mike is afraid of learning to swim but is helped by his father, his
best friend, Lizzie, and a very unusual food.
    ISBN 0-385-32522-3. — ISBN 0-440-41435-0 (pbk.)
    [1. Swimming—Fiction. 2. Fear—Fiction. 3. Food—Fiction.]
I. Demarest, Chris L., II. Title.
PZ7.H3673Mi   1998
[E]—dc21   97-28789
                                                                                        CIP
                                                                                         AC

Visit us on the Web! www.bdd.com
Educators and librarians, visit the BDD Teacher's Resource Center at
www.bdd.com/teachers

Hardcover: The trademark Delacorte Press® is registered in the U.S. Patent and
Trademark Office and in other countries.
Paperback: The trademark Yearling® is registered in the U.S. Patent and
Trademark Office and in other countries.
The text of this book is set in 17-point Baskerville.
Manufactured in the United States of America
June 1998
10 9 8 7 6 5 4 3 2 1

Contents

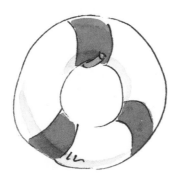

1.

Chocolate-Covered Dust Bunnies

"Mike Swan, where are you?

Oh, there you are!" said Dad.

"Come out from under that bed.

Lizzie is here.

It's time for your swimming lesson."

"No," said Mike. "I'm not going."

"Oh, Mike," said Dad.

"It's so dusty under there.

You're covered with dust bunnies.

Please come out."

Mike looked at his pajamas.

They *were* covered with dust bunnies.

It was gross.

But he shook his head.

"Come on!" said Lizzie.

"It's the first lesson of the year.

Why don't you want to go?"

Lizzie was Mike's best friend.

She already knew how to swim.

"Alligators," said Mike.

Lizzie laughed.

"There are no alligators in the
swimming pool," she said.

"What if there's a hole in the pool?
I might swim to China by mistake."

"Then Lizzie and I will fly over.

We can all eat moo shoo pork," said Dad.

"Mike, what's really bothering you?"

Mike was quiet for a minute.

Then he said, "What if I drown?"

"I don't want you to drown," said Dad.

"That's why you should learn to swim."

"I'm scared, Dad," Mike said.

"What if I say you can have ice cream
after your swimming lesson?" said Dad.
"Say it," said Mike.
"You can have ice cream
after your swimming lesson."
"Can I have ice cream with
chocolate-covered dust bunnies?"
asked Mike.
"Yuck!" Lizzie laughed.

Mike crawled out
from under the bed.
"Dad, don't you ever
sweep under there?
It's gross!"

2.

Wet Heads

The swimming pool was crowded.

"There are a billion kids here.

If I drown nobody will see," said Mike.

"You won't drown," said Dad.

"And I'll be watching you."

"Do you promise?" asked Mike.

"I promise," said Dad.

Mike walked to the shallow end.

He put his towel and shirt on a bench.

Lizzie walked to the other end.

She was with the real swimmers.

Mike watched Lizzie jump in.

She swam to the other side.

Mike was the same age as Lizzie.

Why couldn't he swim too?

It didn't look hard.

It was just so scary!

A lifeguard walked up to Mike.

"Hey, buddy, what's your name?"

he asked.

"Mike Swan."

"Swan, huh?

I bet you love the water!

My name is Sam. I'm your teacher."

Mike looked over at Dad.

Mike shook his head.

"Ice cream," Dad yelled.

"Ice cream," said Mike.

"Ice cream?" Sam asked.

"I love ice cream!

But not in the pool."

Somebody blew a whistle.

"Everybody in the water," said Sam.

All the other kids jumped right in.

Mike walked slowly down the steps.

"Today we're going to put our heads
in the water," said Sam.

"I can do that," said a freckled girl.

"That's easy!"

She held her nose and dunked.

One by one the other kids
put their heads in the water.

"Mike," said Sam. "It's your turn."

Mike was not going to dunk his head.

No way.

What if he couldn't breathe?

Just then someone bumped into Mike.
His feet slipped out from under him.
His head went under the water.
Mike was scared.

He held his breath.

His feet found the pool floor.

He popped right up out of the water.

"Way to go, Mike!" said Sam.

The lesson was over.

Sam gave each kid a badge

to sew onto his or her swimsuit.

It said WET HEAD.

They all ran to show their parents.

Mike stuffed his badge in his pocket.
He had gone under the water
by accident.
He was not a real Wet Head.
He was never coming back.
And he didn't even want ice cream.

3.
Peanut Butter and Baloney

"I'm never going back,"
Mike told Lizzie a few days later.
"Why not?" asked Lizzie.
"Because I'll never learn
how to swim."
"Sure you will," said Lizzie.
"Everybody does."

"How?" asked Mike.

"You just get in the water
and go for it," said Lizzie.

"I can't go for it," said Mike.

"That's baloney!" said Lizzie.

"Lunchtime!" shouted
Lizzie's mother.

Mike and Lizzie ran to the kitchen.

"What would you like?"

asked Mrs. Finch.

"We have peanut butter and jelly,

baloney and cheese, and yogurt."

"Peanut butter and jelly," said Lizzie.

"Peanut butter and . . . baloney,"
said Mike.
"Peanut butter and baloney?"
asked Mrs. Finch.
"Are you sure?"
"You can't eat peanut butter
and baloney together," said Lizzie.
"I eat it all the time," said Mike.
"Yuck," said Lizzie.

Mike had never really eaten

a peanut butter and baloney sandwich.

Mrs. Finch gave him his plate.

"Go for it!" said Lizzie.

Mike picked up his sandwich.

It looked gross.

He closed his eyes. He took a bite.

It tasted horrible!

Mike took a gulp of milk.

He took another bite of the sandwich.

Lizzie and her mother stared at him.

Little by little Mike ate the whole

peanut butter and baloney sandwich.

"Wow!" said Lizzie.

Later, Mike told Dad about it.
"Let me tell you something,
Mike Swan," said Dad.
"If you can eat a
peanut butter and baloney sandwich,
you can do anything."

4.
Sink or Swim

The whistle blew.

"Everybody in," yelled Sam.

Mike looked at Dad.

Dad made a thumbs-up sign.

Sam gave each kid a kickboard.
One by one they kicked
across the pool.

Mike watched them.

The other side was so far away.

Then he saw Lizzie.

"Go for it!" she yelled.

"Peanut butter and baloney!"
yelled Dad.

"Peanut butter and baloney?"
asked Sam.

"I love peanut butter and baloney.
That's my favorite kind of sandwich!"

"It *is*?" Mike said.

"Sure is," said Sam.

"But not in the pool."

Mike grabbed on to the kickboard.

He started to kick.

He was scared.

But he kicked and kicked.

He had almost made it across the pool.

Then something terrible happened.

The kickboard flew
out of Mike's hands.
It floated away from him.
Mike had nothing to hold on to.
"This is it," he thought.
"Sink or swim."

Mike pictured Lizzie swimming.

He kicked his legs.

He moved his arms.

"Peanut butter and baloney,"

he said to himself.

"Peanut butter and baloney!"

Mike reached out.

He grabbed on to the wall.

He'd made it!

"You swam!" yelled Lizzie.

"Way to go, Mike," said Sam.

Dad ran over. "You did it!"

Mike looked at Lizzie.

He looked at Dad.

He looked at Sam.

He smiled.

"Boy, am I hungry," he said.

"How about a nice, fat peanut butter
and baloney sandwich?" said Lizzie.
"I've got one right here," said Sam.
"You know," said Mike, "I think
I'll just have some ice cream."
Dad smiled.
"But," said Mike, "don't forget the
chocolate-covered dust bunnies."

A Gift

For:

From:

Other Books by Bradley Trevor Greive

The Blue Day Book

The Blue Day Book for Kids

Dear Mom

Looking for Mr. Right

The Meaning of Life

The Incredible Truth About Mothers

Tomorrow

The Book for People Who Do Too Much

Friends to the End

Dear Dad

The Simple Truth About Love

Friends to the End
for Kids

The True Value of Friendship

BRADLEY TREVOR GREIVE

GIFT BOOKS
from Hallmark

BOK1095

Andrews McMeel
Publishing, LLC

New York Times best-selling author **Bradley Trevor Greive**, author of the modern classic
The Blue Day Book, is a household name in 105 countries. His eleven previous books have won awards
worldwide and sold more than twelve million copies. Born in Tasmania, Bradley spent most of his childhood
living in the United Kingdom, Hong Kong, and Singapore. A graduate of Australia's Royal Military College, he
served as a paratroop platoon commander before leaving the army to pursue more
creative misadventures. Also an award-winning artist, cartoonist, poet, screenwriter, rock-lifting
champion, and qualified cosmonaut, Bradley lives mostly in Sydney, Australia.

Friends to the End
for Kids

Trying to talk about our friendship is like chewing
ten pieces of bubble gum at the same time—
it ties my tongue up in knots.

It's really hard to get out
all the words to explain how good it feels
to be your friend,

which is pretty weird, because talking
is one of the things we do best.

But lately I've been thinking a lot
about friendship

and about what makes it so great
to have good friends.

For one thing,
friends truly care about each other.

You can trust them
with your most secret secrets,

and you can count on them to watch your back

and never forget about you
or leave you behind.

It's kind of spooky, but friends
just seem to know what you need
without even saying a word,

whether it's a big hug,

an emergency back scratch,

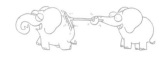

or just a little peace and quiet
to get your thoughts together.

Of course, it's also good to have some
time alone with your favorite toys

or a pig-out snack attack.

But when a friend calls,

 you slam on the brakes, turn around,

and then come running
as fast as you can.

Because with friends (and this is the best
thing about friendship), spending time
with each other means fun—loads of fun!

It might mean putting on a hilarious
musical production in fancy costumes

or splashing around in the pool
or at the beach on a hot day.

Friends have fun going on
crazy adventures,

catching the first summer raindrops or
winter snowflakes on the tips of their tongues,

and singing (or screaming at the top of
their lungs) all the words to their favorite songs.

One day you might start out inventing
strange, delicious cookies in the kitchen

and end up doing wild and crazy dances
till you are absolutely wiped out.

27

Of course, every friendship has rough spots, too.

There will be times when we don't see eye-to-eye.
Big arguments can start over silly things.

We might even make the mistake
of letting others come between us.
And that would make me sad.

The truth is that even the best friends
can drive each other crazy from time to time

or do things that are way too gross to believe.

But eventually, we have to shrug our shoulders,
forgive each other, and move on,

 because that's what real friends do.

Without friends, life would be
awfully lonely, perhaps a little bit scary,
and certainly a lot more boring.

 After all, you can't do high-fives with yourself
without looking like an idiot.

Sometimes even really fun things
don't seem worth doing
without someone to share them with,

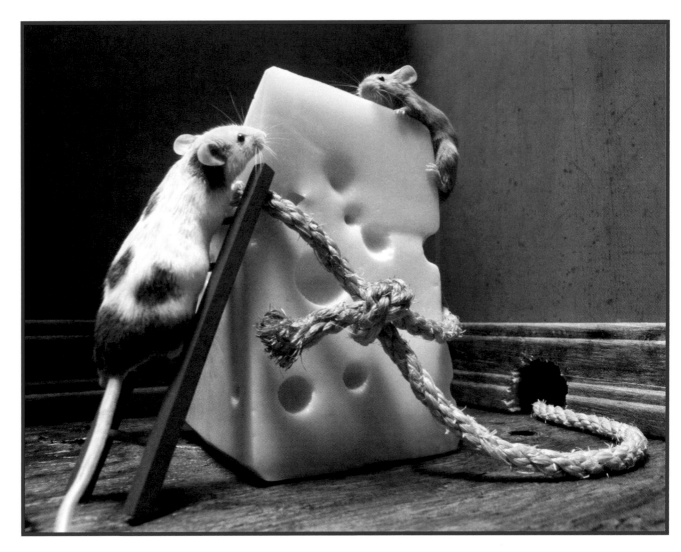

and, what's more, with friends we can do
so many things that we just can't do by ourselves.
In fact, with their help, even the
utterly impossible
seems deliciously doable.

True friends make us smile as soon as we see them.

 They brighten up our day without even trying—
it just feels good to have them around.

I know how lucky I am
to have found a friend like you.

And I just want to say that no matter what happens,
you will never be alone,

because I will always be your friend.

Always.

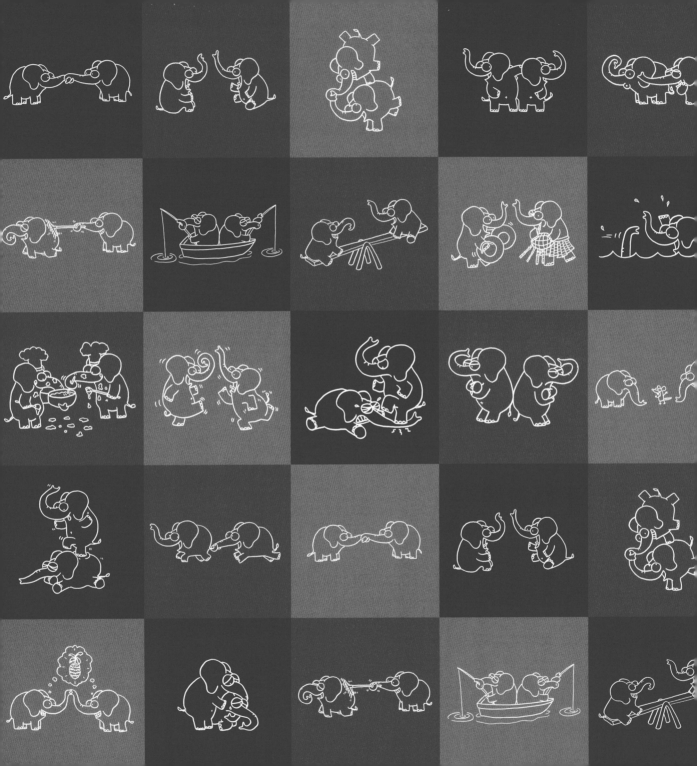